Sassy
The Birthday Storm

Sassy
The Birthday Storm

Sharon M. Draper

SCHOLASTIC INC.
New York   Toronto   London   Auckland
Sydney   Mexico City   New Delhi   Hong Kong

This book was originally published in hardcover
by Scholastic Press in 2009.

ISBN-13: 978-0-545-07156-7
ISBN-10: 0-545-07156-9

12 11 10 9 8 7 6 5 4 3   10 11 12 13 14/0

Printed in the U.S.A.   40
First Scholastic paperback printing, November 2009

Book design by Elizabeth B. Parisi

This book is dedicated to
Landon Charles Draper,
who loves animals and
the beach, and all things
bright and beautiful.
—SD

CHAPTER ONE

Digging for Pink

"**M**om! I can't find my pink swimsuit!"

A huge pile of clothes seems to live on the floor of my closet. I dig and find my favorite yellow shorts, one torn plastic sandal, two pairs of jeans, and a shiny silver belt.

I also find several pairs of underwear and my lost gym clothes. But it seems my pink swimsuit has moved away.

"You don't need it. Take your green bathing suit instead," my mother answers from down the hall.

"I hate the green one!" I tell her. "It looks like an army uniform."

My sixteen-year-old sister, Sadora, sticks her head in my door. She has been packed and ready since yesterday.

"Wear some big army boots and your green swimsuit will look great," she teases.

"We're going to the *beach*!" I yell.

"I know that. Maybe the beach people will think you're starting a new fashion trend."

She comes into my room. I'm sitting on the floor with clothes on my head.

Usually, Sadora can make me giggle, but today I don't feel like laughing. "I just gotta have that pink suit," I tell her.

"Why?" she asks.

"You won't understand," I tell her.

"Try me," she says. Sometimes my big sister can be really cool.

I wrinkle my face and think. "Because when I wear that bathing suit, the sun is always warm and bright, no rain ever falls on the beach, and I find the perfect seashell for my collection."

"So it's like your good-luck suit?" she asks.

"Yeah, something like that," I tell her. "And besides, it goes with my lucky pink ribbon." I tie it carefully around my puffy ponytail.

"I understand about matching," Sadora says. "But what's lucky about that ribbon?" Sadora asks.

"Because it was at the bottom of my Sassy Sack when Grammy gave it to me!" I explain. "Good things happen when I wear it."

Sadora shakes her head. "Did you look in your dirty-clothes hamper?" she asks. She sits on my bed next to my overstuffed suitcase.

"It's not there," I say.

"What about your bottom drawer?" Sadora asks. "Isn't that your pink drawer? Don't you have a system where you arrange your clothes by color?"

"I gave that up," I tell her glumly. "It was too complicated."

But I pull out the bottom drawer and look anyway. I find a pair of rose-colored socks and a sparkly pink hair barrette but no pink swimsuit.

My twelve-year-old brother, Sabin, bursts into the room. He's wearing the new sunglasses he bought last night at the drugstore.

"You don't need the shades in the house," I remind him.

"I'm going to keep them on for the entire trip," he says. "Maybe some Florida girls will think I'm a movie star!"

He looks at himself in my mirror. He turns his baseball cap so the visor is in the back. He's wearing a new red T-shirt, and his skinny arms look like thin tree branches sticking out.

I giggle. "Which movie did you star in? The Tooth-pick Man?"

Sadora cracks up.

Sabin ignores both of us and grabs a candy bar from my bed.

"Sabin! I was gonna eat that on the plane!" I tell him as I reach for the candy.

"Not this one," he says with a grin as he takes off the wrapper. "Maybe it will help me build muscles." He gobbles it in two bites.

I don't tell Sabin, but I have three more candy bars in my Sassy Sack. They are hiding in a zipper pocket, far away from a big brother's greedy fingers.

My Sassy Sack is the coolest thing. It's more than a purse. It's like a part of me. Just touching it makes me feel happy. It's pink and purple and shiny and made of lots of different fabrics, like lace and silk and velvet. It's got buttons and sparkles and it closes with a satin ribbon.

Sadora rubs her hands over my sack. "Grammy gave this to you for your seventh birthday, didn't she?" she asks with a smile.

"Yep. It's one of a kind and I love it. I don't go anyplace without it. You know that," I tell her.

"So what are you going to give Grammy for *her* birthday?" Sadora asks.

"It's a surprise," I say. "You'll see when we get there."

Sabin finishes the candy and burps. "Dad says to give me

your suitcase so I can put it in the car. And he says hurry up. We're gonna miss the plane!"

"You can't take it yet," I cry out. "I'm still packing."

But he zips my bag shut, snatches it off my bed, and hurries out the door with it.

"Sabin!" I yell. But he's gone. I can hear him clumping down the stairs.

"My swimsuit must be invisible," I tell Sadora with a sigh.

"Grammy never notices what we wear. She just loves it because we're there," Sadora says. She sounds wise, like a grown-up.

"I know Grammy doesn't care about my clothes," I tell Sadora. "But do you think she'll like my new outfit anyway?"

Sadora laughs. "You're impossible, Little Sister. Of course Grammy will like your new purple hookup. And Poppy won't even notice! You look like a piece of grape candy."

"That's my favorite!" I tell her with a grin.

I look at myself in the mirror. I'm wearing a pale purple T-shirt with shiny silver writing on the front. It says BEACH BUM. My shorts and socks are a light shade of lavender. My shoes and shoelaces are purple. Only my hair ribbon is hot pink.

Sadora is right. I look like a Popsicle!

"You look super, Sassy," Sadora tells me. "I would have worn that same outfit when I was nine and a half."

That makes me feel really good. "Thanks," I tell her.

"Why don't you add a belt?" she suggests.

"Great idea!" From my top drawer I pull a shiny purple belt. It has a huge silver buckle.

"Perfect!" Sadora tells me as I put on the belt.

"Sassy! Sadora! Let's go!" Mom calls from the bottom of the stairs. "If we miss the plane, we miss Grammy's birthday celebration. Hurry!"

I take one last look around my room, grab my Sassy Sack, and turn off the light. I dig down into my sack to make sure I have a book to read on the plane. I feel something soft.

I pull it out, and rolled into a ball is my shiny pink swimsuit. "I found it!" I yell with relief. "I forgot that I put it in my sack!"

Sadora pats me on the shoulder. "I'm glad you found it, Little Sister. That's the kind of thing that can spoil a trip." We head down the stairs together.

"This is going to be the best Florida trip ever!" I tell her as we rush out of the door and into the car.

"Grammy's birthday on the beach! I can't wait," Sadora says happily.

CHAPTER TWO

Hurry Up and Wait

"Is everybody ready for this beach vacation?" Daddy asks with a smile on his face. He's wearing a blue shirt with red flowers on it.

"Good grief!" Sadora whispers to me. "Look at what Daddy has on! I hope I don't see anybody I know at the airport."

"Ready!" we all shout. Everybody loves going to Grammy's house. We live in Ohio, and Grammy and Poppy live in Florida in a really cool beach house.

"I love getting up every morning seeing the ocean," Sadora tells me.

"Yep, and this year we're going to be there in time for Grammy's birthday. Even better," I say.

"You know, there's a tropical depression swirling in the Atlantic," Daddy warns as we load stuff into the car.

"What's depressing about the tropics?" Sabin asks. "Seems like everybody there ought to be happy all the time!"

"A tropical depression is an organized system of clouds and winds and storms," Daddy explains. "Sometimes it fizzles in the ocean, but sometimes it gets stronger and turns into what we call a tropical storm." Daddy is a science teacher. He likes to answer scientific questions.

"Is that bad?" Sadora asks.

"Well, that would mean it might rain on our birthday celebration," Mom replies. "But a tropical storm can get really strong sometimes, and it becomes a hurricane!"

"Hurricane?" Sabin and Sadora and I all say the word at the same time.

"Storms and hurricanes are very unpredictable," Daddy reassures us. "We'll probably be just fine."

"Probably?" I whisper. Nobody hears me as we climb into our car.

As usual, I'm squeezed in the backseat between Sabin and Sadora. Sabin smells like his favorite Ocean Breeze aftershave lotion.

"Did you use a whole bottle of that stuff, Sabin?" I ask, pretending to cough a little. "You don't even shave!"

He just leans closer to me and laughs.

Sadora smells like roses. I hope I don't choke on the smells before we get to the airport. I reach down into my sack and pull out a small portable minifan. But instead of making the smells go away, it just blows them around and mixes them. I give up and put the fan away.

"Are you sorry your friend Jasmine is not able to be with us?" Sadora asks.

Jasmine is my very best friend and she could be sitting here with me, giggling about Sadora's bracelets, or Sabin's big feet, or what we could buy in the airport gift shop.

I explain to Sadora, "Too bad she has a music competition this week. I will have *too* much to tell her when I get home!"

I sit back, cross my arms across my chest, and sigh. Sabin, shades on his eyes and earbuds in his ears, is bopping his head to the music on his iPod. He gazes out of the window on the right side.

Sadora, who always looks like she's ready to star in a movie, looks out of the window on the left side.

All I have to look at is the back of the seat in front of me. And all I can think about is the storm that might be coming.

"Daddy?" I ask quietly as he stops at a red light.

"Yes, Sassy?" he answers without turning around.

"Hurricanes are pretty terrible, aren't they?"

"Not necessarily, Little Sister," Daddy says as the light turns green. "Hurricanes are divided into five categories.

A Category One storm has the lowest wind speeds, while a Category Five hurricane has the strongest."

"Now we've got to listen to the Daddy Weather Channel all the way to the airport," Sadora hisses at me.

All of us know that Daddy sometimes doesn't know when to stop answering the question.

Daddy looks at me through the rearview mirror and winks. He explains, "A Category One has winds that are at least seventy-four miles per hour."

"Can that spoil a beach party?" I ask.

"Absolutely," Mom says.

"There would be lots of rain and wind, and maybe some flooding," Daddy continues. "A Category Two hurricane carries winds up to a hundred and ten miles per hour, while a Category Five, the most intense, would involve winds of well over a hundred and fifty miles per hour, and for sure there would be lots and lots of destruction."

"Wow," I whisper. "That would be terrible."

"Hurricane Katrina was a Four or a Five, wasn't it, Dad?" Sabin asks.

"Yes, son, it was one of the worst," Daddy replies with a sigh.

The whole family is quiet for the rest of the drive to the airport.

When we finally get there, Daddy has a hard time

finding a parking place. I'm amazed that there are so many cars waiting in the dreary space for their owners to return.

As we climb out of our car and start to unload our bags, I touch it to say good-bye. I know it's silly, but I feel sorry that the car has to sit in that cold, gray, dingy garage for a whole week while we have fun on the beach.

I don't tell Sadora what I'm thinking, though. She'll think I'm nuts!

As we head to the check-in area of the airport, I look at my family and wonder what a stranger would think of us.

Mom drags two small beige bags behind her. She walks tall and proud, even when she's relaxed and on vacation. Mom is dressed all in green. She likes for her clothes to match. She is wearing green sandals, a pale green sundress, and plastic earrings that look like emeralds.

Mom smiles at Daddy. "We didn't forget anything, did we, Sam?"

He's dragging two huge black bags on wheels. "I think our whole house is with us!" he jokes. "Did you pack the living room sofa in this bag?" He wipes sweat from his forehead.

"No, just the chair and the rugs," Mom replies with a grin.

Sabin wears his school book bag slung over one shoulder and pulls a blue backpack on wheels.

"Turn off that music player for now, Sabin," Daddy says to him.

He doesn't hear him and keeps on walking and bopping to the music.

Mom touches Sabin's arm. "Music off!" she says.

"Huh?" He looks like he just came back to this planet.

Sadora laughs and pulls the earbuds from his ears. "Mom says for you to chill for a minute," she tells him.

Sabin rolls his eyes, but he turns off the music player.

"I hope Mom checked your suitcase before we left, Sabin," I tell him.

"How come?"

"Because you always forget something important, like underwear or deodorant," I remind him.

"I'm cool," he says. "I've got my candy and chips. I won't need much more than that."

Sadora and I just shake our heads.

Sadora is dressed in white shorts and an orange top. She looks really pretty, but I'd never tell her that.

She wears a small, neat backpack and pulls her new blue-and-white suitcase. Sadora always gets new stuff and I get her leftovers. That's so not fair!

So I'm dragging my overstuffed pink suitcase that used to be my sister's. It's a little beat-up, and a little dirty, but I like it because it has sparkles and shiny flowers on it.

And I carry my wonderful Sassy Sack. In it I have stuff I need like tissues and brushes and shiny new pencils, but also cool stuff like nail polish and lip gloss and lotion.

When we get inside the airport, I can see why Daddy was in such a hurry to get here on time. There must be a zillion people ahead of us in line.

We already have our tickets because Daddy printed them out from our computer. But we have to check our bags.

"I hate waiting," I whine to Mom. I shift from one foot to the other.

"Be patient, Sassy," Mom says.

I take a big breath. I look at my watch. I sit on my suitcase. I stand. I sit again. I sigh.

Sabin plays a video game. Sadora reads a teen magazine. I pick the polish off my nails.

I reach into my sack and get some lip gloss for the fifth time. My lips are greasy with gloss.

It takes twenty-seven minutes before it is our turn to go to the desk and check our bags. The lady at the counter is very nice, though. As she is putting the tags on our bags, she tells me my outfit is cute.

"And that's a lovely pink ribbon you're wearing," the woman adds. She doesn't say anything to Sadora at all. That makes all the waiting worth it.

CHAPTER THREE
Crazy Security!

We finally get our bags checked, our boarding passes in hand, and we head for still another long line. I'm tired, and we're not even on the plane yet.

The security line is crazy. First we have to take off our shoes and put them in little gray bins with our backpacks and jackets and purses.

"Why do we have to take off our shoes?" Sabin asks Daddy. "My feet are cold!"

"You always have to remove your shoes, Sabin," Mom tells him, using her patient "mother" voice. "You know that."

Daddy looks at Sabin's bare feet. "Where are your socks, Sabin?" he asks.

"I forgot them."

"I knew you would forget something!" I tell Sabin with a laugh.

His big, naked feet look really out of place on that cold cement floor. I almost feel sorry for him.

Mom and Daddy laugh at him. I hold my nose and pretend his feet stink. Sadora tries to act like she doesn't know him.

Everybody in my family gets through the line with no trouble. Mom goes first, walking through the little doorway when a security guard motions to her. The green light says she's safe.

Sadora breezes through the line with no blips. The security guards smile at her and wish her a safe trip.

Sabin, bare feet and all, clomps through the little doorway. The green light flashes for him. He hurries to find his shoes in the gray bin on the other side of the X-ray machine that takes pictures of the inside of our stuff.

Daddy has to take off his belt and his cell phone, but he also goes through with no trouble.

My family, on the other side of the security section, put on their shoes and jackets and jewelry.

Mom says, "Come on, Sassy. It's almost time for our flight!"

Finally, it's my turn. I walk through the little doorway and a bell rings.

Bing! Bing! Bing!

I look around in confusion.

"What's wrong?" I ask.

"Excuse me, ma'am," a security guard says. He's wearing a uniform with a white shirt and blue pants. It looks a little like my school uniform except it has writing on the shirt.

I can't believe somebody is calling me ma'am! I'm in the fourth grade.

"Excuse me, ma'am," he says again. "Would you walk through once more, please?"

I back up, take a deep breath, and walk very slowly toward the security entrance. I can see my family on the other side. But when I walk through, it happens again.

Bing! Bing! Bing!

"What did I do?" I ask. I'm getting scared. Maybe everybody will go to Florida to see Grammy and I'll have to sleep in the airport for a week all by myself.

The man in the white shirt says to me, "Walk this way, miss. I'll have to check you by hand. There is nothing to worry about."

But I'm worried anyway.

Mom calls to me from the safe area. "It's okay, Sassy. This will only take a minute."

Daddy gives me a thumbs-up sign.

Sabin is cracking up, so Daddy bops him on the shoulder to tell him to stop.

Sadora knows I'm scared. I can see it on her face. She waves and tries to make me smile. I can't.

The security man takes me to a little glassed-in area and says, "Please stand here."

I see two footprints on a plastic mat. I put one foot on each of the footprints, but my feet are little and the footprints are big enough for a giant.

I don't have my shoes on, so the mat feels squishy under my socks.

"I'm going to use this wand to check you, okay?" he says gently. He sounds nice, but I'm still scared.

I nod. The only wands I know about are in stories about magic princesses. They are pink and sparkly, and they turn frogs into handsome princes.

The thing in his hand looks nothing like that. It's black and wide and it makes a beeping noise like something from one of Sabin's video games. *Ding! Ping!*

The security man and his wand do not touch me, but he runs the wand over my head, down each arm, and behind my back and front.

It beeps loudly when it gets close to my waist. *Ding! Ping!*

"That's a very pretty belt you're wearing," the man says. "Your silver buckle is the reason for the beep."

I do not say thank you. I'm too scared.

The security man moves the wand over my head. *Ding! Ping!*

"Is that a metal barrette in your hair?" he asks.

"Yes, sir," I reply. I can see my mother on the other side. I want to run to her. She blows me a kiss. I'm too nervous to pretend to catch it.

"I think that's what caused the machine to ding this time," the security guard explains.

"Should I take it off?" I ask him.

"No, you're fine. Have a nice trip." He walks away.

I remove the barrette anyway. I don't think I'll ever wear it again.

I hurry to the area where my shoes are waiting for me. Mom gives me a hug.

"That was horrible!" I tell her. "I felt like a criminal."

"You were very brave, sweetie," she says. Her voice sounds soothing.

I'm glad my family is close to me. Even Sabin's Ocean Breeze cologne smells good now.

"Let's get to our gate," Daddy says cheerfully then.

"Amen!" I say.

I put on my shoes, the purple ones with the purple sparkly laces, and I look for my Sassy Sack. It's not there.

"Where's my sack?" I ask with alarm.

Another security person comes up to me then, holding

my sack like it was something ordinary. She is wearing blue plastic gloves. "Does this belong to you?" she asks me. Her voice sounds stern and not very friendly at all.

"Yes!" I tell her. I reach for my bag, but she holds it up so I can't get to it.

"I'm going to have to look through it," she says.

"No!" I say. My purse is very special to me and *nobody* is allowed to look in it, not even my mom.

The woman looks mean. She does not smile. "If you don't let me examine the contents of the bag, you cannot take it on the plane," she says in a harsh voice.

I look to my mother for help. I feel like I'm going to cry.

Mom walks over to me and puts her hand on my shoulder. "It's okay, Sassy. This happens to me all the time when I travel. They won't hurt your stuff."

"But it's *personal*, Mom," I try to explain. "What's in there is nobody's business but mine."

"I understand, Sassy," Mom says. "You don't have to be embarrassed. These people have probably seen a little of everything."

"No, you *don't* understand!" I tell her desperately. "It's not like I have anything bad or embarrassing — it's just that the stuff in my bag belongs to *me*! It's supposed to be private and special. Why does she have to go through my things?" I stomp my feet.

"Just relax, sweetie," Mom says in her soothing voice.

But I don't feel soothed at all. "No fair!" I tell her angrily.

"Let's just see what caused the machine to make them notice your Sassy Sack. You have so much stuff in there."

The security woman takes her gloved hand and starts to dig around in my sack. I feel like she is digging into my body.

She pulls out my six ink pens, all in different glow-in-the-dark colors. Pansy Pink. Gala Green. Cherry Red. Banana Yellow. Juicy Orange. And Passion Purple. She sets them in one of the little gray bins.

Then she pulls out my markers, my notebooks, my whistle, my mirror, and my flashlight. I'm feeling like I want to throw up. This is my special stuff, and she's touching it and looking at it.

She takes out my bracelets, my earrings, and my special good-luck key ring that Grammy gave me on her last trip to my house. She removes my camera, my book, and even my pink swimsuit.

"You've got quite a bit in here, young lady," she says to me.

I don't answer her, and I don't smile at her. I want her to stop.

When the woman gets to little bottles of nail polish, lotion, and hand sanitizer, she sets them in a different bin. "You must place these items in a small plastic bag for them to go through security," she tells me.

"Why?"

"Because that's the rule," the woman replies.

"What if I don't have a plastic bag?"

"Then these things will have to be thrown away," the security woman explains.

"So if I put my nail polish in a plastic bag, it's safe to travel with, but if I just have it in my purse, it's not allowed."

"Correct," the woman says. She glares at me.

"I don't get it. That makes no sense to me at all." I glare back at her.

Mom reaches down into her purse and pulls out an empty plastic bag. "I'm sorry, Sassy. I should have known you'd need this. Here, let's place these things in the bag."

"That's better," the security woman says when she sees I have the lotion, polish, and hand sanitizer safely in plastic.

The security woman keeps digging in my sack. Finally, she finds a fat tube of coconut-scented hair gel. She says, "Here is your problem. You cannot take this on the plane. It contains more than three ounces of liquid."

"But how am I gonna fix my hair?" I ask. "This is the only stuff that makes my hair behave."

"You can go back out and check you hair gel as luggage," the woman says. "But then you'll have to go through the security line again."

"No way!" I tell her.

"Just toss the hair gel," Mom tells the woman. The lady throws my hair gel into a trash can. I notice the garbage is full of water bottles and cans of soda and hair spray and other items I guess people couldn't take on the plane.

"What a waste!" I whisper to Mom.

The woman looks at me then and asks, "Would you like me to return your items to your purse or do you want to do it?"

"I'll do it!" I tell her loudly. Slowly and carefully, I put my stuff back into my sack. Mom seems to understand I'm upset, so she doesn't rush me, but I can see she is checking her watch.

"Sassy!" I hear Sadora say. "Come on!"

"Hurry up, Little Sister!" Sabin calls.

I know it's getting close to the time for our flight to leave, so I toss the rest of the things in my sack and throw the strap over my shoulder. It doesn't even feel the same against my body. It's lumpy where it wasn't before and uneven in places where it had been smooth.

I'm glad the flight takes two hours. It's going to take me that long to make things right again.

CHAPTER FOUR

Up in the Air and Down Again

The plane is huge. As we walk down the narrow aisle to row twenty-one, I start to relax and feel excited once more. The seats are arranged with three on one side of the aisle and three on the other side.

Sabin gets to our row first, so he rushes in and takes the window seat.

"Sabin!" I cry out. "No fair! I never get to sit by the window!"

He grins at me and says, "Maybe you'll get lucky on the flight home!"

I can tell he's not going to move, so I slide in and take the middle seat, as usual. Sadora takes the seat on the aisle.

Daddy is sitting in the aisle seat across from us. Mom has the middle seat, just like me. I wave to her as we get our seat belts on.

We finally get settled and the safety video is shown. The plane backs up, then revs up, then takes off into the sky. I wish I could see more, but Sabin blocks most of the view as he gazes out the window.

"Awesome!" he says. "Better than a video game!"

He finally sits back, and when the flight attendant says it's okay, Sabin puts his earbuds back in, cranks up his iPod, and closes his eyes.

Sadora puts down her movie star magazine and says to me, "I know you feel bad about the security people going through your sack. I bet you felt like screaming!"

I hug my bag close to me. "Yeah, I did. How can a little girl's purse be dangerous?" I ask her.

Sadora has no answer to that. "Did she put her hands on *everything*?" she asks me.

"No, lots of things in the inside zipper pockets she didn't even see." I giggle. "What if that lady got my superglue all over her fingers?"

We both laugh. "Your sack is pretty awesome, Sassy."

"I'm going to fix it and arrange it when we get to Grammy and Poppy's house," I tell Sadora. "Grammy will help me."

"Are you excited about Grammy's birthday party on Thursday?" Sadora asks.

"Oh, yeah! Grammy says she's having hula dancers and a limbo contest!"

"And Poppy told me he hired a live band that plays beach music," Sadora reminds me. "We'll dance on the beach!"

"And the food," Sabin adds. "Lots and lots of food."

"I didn't know you were listening," I tell him.

"I always pay attention when it comes to eating," Sabin says with a grin. He takes the earbud from his left ear. "Poppy says he's grilling hot dogs and hamburgers."

"And barbecue," Sadora adds.

"And Grammy's potato salad and baked beans and roasted corn on the cob," Sabin says.

"Don't forget the cake!" I remind them. "Grammy says it's huge!"

"I bet it has a million candles on it," Sabin says with a laugh.

"Don't let Grammy hear you say that," Sadora warns him. "I sure hope it doesn't rain," she says with a sigh.

"Or anything worse — like a hurricane," Sabin adds.

"Why do you think they give hurricanes names?" I ask them.

Sadora tells me, "Hurricanes used to be named after girls, but now they are given names of both girls and boys."

"I looked up the names on the Internet before we left," Sabin says. "They start with the letter A and end with the letter W."

"What's wrong with X, Y, and Z?" I ask.

"Q, U, X, Y, and Z are never used," he replies. "I guess there aren't enough names with those letters."

"Well, I guess we'll never have a Hurricane Zippy," Sadora says with a laugh.

"Maybe if we don't talk about it or think about it, nothing will happen," I tell her.

"I hope you're right, Little Sister," Sadora tells me as the flight attendant gives us little plastic glasses of Coke.

I'm still thirsty when I finish my teeny little soda, but I'm afraid to ask for more. Instead, I get a peppermint stick out of my sack. But it just makes me thirstier.

When a flight attendant rushes past our row, I raise my hand, but since I'm little, and I'm sitting in the middle, she never notices me. She walks past our row six more times. Each time I raise my hand, and each time she doesn't see me.

"Did you want something?" Sadora asks.

"I'm really thirsty," I admit.

Sadora gives me the rest of her Coke. That's pretty cool of her. I drink it all and suck on the ice until it's gone.

"You know, Grammy always gives us the perfect gift for our birthdays," I say to my sister and brother. "Do we have enough special stuff to give to her?"

"I bought her two new CDs," Sabin says. "She likes music."

"I bought her something really cool," Sadora says. "It's an electronic picture frame. It displays lots of pictures of us on a screen. She plugs it in and she can see us even when we are back at home in Ohio."

I am starting to feel bad. I didn't buy Grammy anything. But I did bring her a present. I hope it's good enough.

"What did you buy for Grammy, Little Sister?" Sabin asks.

"It's a surprise," I say. "Just wait and see." I get my book out of my sack and read until it's time to land.

When the plane finally touches down with a bump and a thud, I'm excited. We grab our stuff, I make sure I have my Sassy Sack, and we head out of the plane and into the new airport.

It blows me away that just a little while ago we were in another airport in another state, and now we are here in Florida. The people look different here. They look happy and relaxed.

I whisper to Sabin, "Everybody here seems to be wearing flowered shirts like Daddy!"

"He'll fit right in," he tells me with a chuckle.

My grandmother waits for us at the bottom of the escalator near the baggage claim. She is wearing a long, flowing white sundress and white sandals. Her arms are stretched out in welcome.

"She looks like a grandmother angel," I tell Sadora as the moving stairs take us to Grammy.

"Grammy!" we all cry out as we get to her. She swallows us in her hugs.

"Where's Poppy?" Sabin asks.

"He's teaching a summer class at the university," Grammy tells Sabin. "But he's like you, Sabin. Poppy pops up when it's dinnertime!"

Sabin nods with understanding.

"Happy almost birthday, Mother," my mom says.

"We have three days before the big day," Grammy says as she hugs my mom and dad. "I'm SO glad all of you made it safely. How was your flight?"

"Great!" Sadora tells her.

"Long!" I reply.

"I'm hungry!" Sabin says.

Everybody laughs.

"Let's go get our luggage," Daddy says. "I think we can all use a little unwinding on the beach this afternoon."

We head to the huge carousel that goes around and around with dozens of suitcases. Blue and black and red and spotted. All the passengers claim their bags. Amazingly, all of our bags show up.

Daddy and Sabin pull them off one at a time. My bag is the very last one to come around the circle. And one wheel is missing.

"What happened to my suitcase?" I shriek.

"It happens sometimes," Mom says in her soothing voice.

"Look at it this way," Sadora tells me. "You get to go shopping to buy a new one!"

"But I can't pull it," I complain. The bag drags on one side as I try to move it across the carpet.

"I'll just pick it up and carry it for you," Sabin offers.

"Hmm . . . Wait a minute," I tell him. I dig down into my Sassy Sack until my fingers reach what I'm looking for. I pull out a small toy truck that Jasmine's little brother had tossed in there a couple of weeks ago, and a roll of bandage tape.

"What are you gonna do with that?" Sadora asks. "We're in a hurry, Sassy."

But I sit on the floor, tape the little truck to the broken place where the wheel used to be, and in a moment my suitcase is wobbly but rolls. "Now we can go!" I announce with pride. "And I still get to buy a new one before we go back to Ohio."

Sadora just shakes her head. Grammy smiles at me with pride, however. That makes me feel good.

Grammy is a professional storyteller and she travels all over the world. I guess she must know a zillion people. Lots of folks in the airport seem to know her. They wave and call out her name.

"Good to see you, Miss Sahara!" says a luggage handler.

"It's Sahara Senegal, Mommy! She came to my school!" a little girl calls out with excitement.

Grammy nods and waves and greets everyone with a smile.

Daddy says, "We're ready to roll, family." We pull our luggage, including my patched-up bag, toward the door. A couple of people stop and point, but I don't care.

"I'm so excited I think I might pop," I tell Sadora.

We leave the airport and the hot air hits me in the face like a slap. "Wow!" I say. "This feels like an oven. I can't wait to get in the water!"

"How's the weather, Sahara?" my dad asks Grammy.

Grammy tells him, "It's been very hot lately. But the weather people are a little worried about that storm system that seems to be circling out in the ocean."

We are almost to Grammy's car. I'm already sweating. "Is it getting worse?" I ask with concern.

"A very large tropical storm might be heading this way," Grammy says. Her voice is very serious.

"What kind of tropical storm?" I ask.

"A hurricane," Grammy replies.

CHAPTER FIVE

Warm Sand and Cool Water

"There's really going to be a hurricane?" I say with dread.

Grammy doesn't seem real worried. "Well, these summer storms are unpredictable. Sometimes they veer to the west. Sometimes they decide to go east. And sometimes they just fizzle out and all we get is rain."

Daddy loads our stuff into the back of Grammy's SUV and we climb in. Grammy cranks up the air-conditioning and I feel like I can breathe again.

"What does this storm look like it might do?" Mom asks when we are all settled.

"I checked the Weather Channel before we left," Daddy says, "and nothing is sure yet."

"Is this what you were talking about before we left home?" I ask Daddy.

"Yes, but I wasn't going to let it spoil our plans for Grammy's birthday celebration."

"We haven't had a big storm hit here in several years," Grammy says as she drives. "Lots of threats but no direct hits."

I sit in the third row of seats and I finally have a window to look out of! Florida houses look different somehow. Lots of them seem to be made of stone or brick instead of wood like our house. I'm always amazed at the palm trees that grow here like maple trees grow in Ohio.

"What will happen if the hurricane comes here?" I ask.

"We'll have to wait and see, Sassy," she tells me.

"And what about your birthday party, Grammy?" Sadora wants to know.

Grammy chuckles. "I'll have my birthday with or without a party. I'll still be one year older."

We finally pull into Poppy and Grammy's driveway. Tall palm trees line the path to their house.

"The trees look like soldiers with funny hats," I tell Sadora.

"You're silly," she replies. I like it when she is in a good mood.

Grammy and Poppy's house sits high on a hill. It's large and white and made of stone. And in the distance I can see the ocean.

"It's still there!" I whisper.

"You think the ocean moved away?" Sabin asks with a laugh.

"Of course not," I tell him. "It's just nice to know it's always there — smooth and blue and beautiful."

We unload our gear and drag it all into the house, which is cool and breezy.

"Welcome!" Grammy says to all of us. "This is going to be my best birthday celebration ever. I'm glad that you are here to share it with me."

I go to Grammy and give her another big hug. She always smells like vanilla ice cream.

"I brought you something special for your birthday, Grammy," I tell her quietly.

"If it comes from my Sassy girl, I know it will be wonderful," she tells me. "And I see you wore your lucky pink ribbon."

I'm glad she notices.

I feel peaceful in Poppy and Grammy's house. She has painted everything in tones of pale blue and peach. Soft music plays in the background. And the ocean dances in the distance.

We all sit down to sandwiches and lemonade at their big dining room table. I realize I'm really, really hungry. Even Sadora gobbles all her lunch, and she's a very picky eater. Sabin, of course, eats like a starving elephant.

"How do you stay so thin, Sabin?" Grammy asks with a chuckle. She offers him a plate of brownies. He takes four of them.

"Basketball and track!" he replies with his mouth full.

Just as Sabin is about to reach for another sweet treat, a deep, booming voice calls from the doorway, "I hope somebody left the last brownie for me!"

"Poppy!" we all cry out. Sabin reaches Poppy first and hugs him with chocolate-covered fingers. Sadora and I grab him and hug him tightly, too.

I think Poppy wears a cologne called Grandfather. It smells strong and comfortable, like clothes fresh out of the dryer. He wears a flowered shirt like Daddy wore on the plane, but on Poppy it looks right. He's taller than Daddy and a lot rounder. Poppy has a full head of curly gray hair.

Poppy strides across the room, shakes hands with my father, then gives my mom a special hug. She whispers, "Good to see you, Dad," and I realize she looks at him just like I look at my daddy.

"How's it going at the university?" Mom asks Poppy as he grabs the last brownie and sits down to a sandwich Grammy made for him.

"Just great. I'm planning to take some students to study in Egypt next year. We're going to explore the pyramids!"

"Awesome," Sadora says.

"And I'm going on the trip to gather stories and clothes and shoes!" Grammy adds with a laugh.

After lunch we unpack some of our stuff. Grammy's house is huge. She has three guest rooms. I share the room that has twin beds and twin fans with Sadora. Mom and Daddy share a room.

Sabin will sleep in the loft in the attic. He likes that. "Did you know I can access the Internet from that room?" he tells us. "Way cool. I can surf the net and download some tunes while I'm here."

"If I can pull you from that computer, Sabin, are you ready for some *real* surfing?" Grammy asks with a smile. "Let's get in some beach time."

I can't wait. "Yay!" I say.

I put on my shiny pink swimsuit and pink flip-flops and grab a towel from Grammy's bathroom. I am the first one ready.

I sit in a big soft chair in the living room while I'm waiting for the rest of my family. I love Grammy and Poppy's house. It makes me feel safe and happy.

Sabin, wearing his sunglasses again and long red swim shorts, interrupts my thoughts. "You got any suntan lotion, Sassy?"

I dig down into my sparkly Sassy Sack, pull out a tube of suntan oil, and hand it to him. "Grease up!" I tell him with a laugh.

"Why didn't the security people take this from you?" he asks as he rubs the stuff on his skinny arms and legs.

"It was in my suitcase. I refilled my sack when I got here," I explain.

Sadora comes into the room next. She looks stunning in her white one-piece suit. She looks out of Grammy's huge picture window. "What a perfect day for a swim!" she says.

"It sure doesn't look like a storm is brewing," Sabin says.

I join them at the window. The sky is a clear, bright blue umbrella over a sunny, sparkling beach.

"If I could draw a picture of perfect, that would be it," I tell them.

Mom, Daddy, Poppy, and Grammy, all dressed in swim clothes, join us, and the seven of us head down the path to the beach. Stones have been set in the sand to help us walk easier.

"The air feels like a warm blanket," I say as we get closer to the water.

"Warm blankets and hot days are not a good mix," Sabin jokes.

We spread our towels on the soft white sand, and for a minute I just stand there to look and listen. The sun is golden and hot. The sand is white and sparkly. The water, blue and glistening, goes *whoosh, whoosh* as it rolls onto the beach and then surges back again.

"It's like the ocean is playing a game of Catch Me if You Can," I tell Sadora.

"All day and all night," she replies. "It never stops moving. Up to the sand. Back out again."

"That's crazy!" I tell her.

Sabin is already in the ocean, his skinny arms sticking out of the blue water.

"He looks like a stick fish," I tell Sadora with a giggle.

Suddenly, Sabin runs out of the water, onto the sand, and directly to me and Sadora. He is holding some kind of green plastic toy in his hand.

Before we know it, he has doused both of us with cool ocean water!

"Gotcha!" he says with glee. "I found this toy on the beach. Great for soaking sisters!" He runs in the other direction.

We scream and chase him across the sand. The three of us end up in the ocean, laughing and throwing water on one another.

It feels cold at first, but soon the ocean water seems as warm as bathwater to me. We splash and duck and squeal. We swim and float and bob.

This has gotta be heaven, I think.

"Come on in the water!" I call out to my parents and Grammy and Poppy.

Grammy just motions to us from her beach chair that we should keep on playing, but Daddy and Mom jump up and surprise us by racing each other to the edge of the water. Poppy runs right behind them and passes them both! He holds his arms up high like an Olympic race winner.

Daddy and Mom, breathing hard, laugh as they reach the edge of the water. Poppy runs around both of them in a victory circle, then dives into the ocean with us.

Mom stops and lets the waves cover her ankles and toes. She squeals a little and pretends to be afraid. She's slim and in pretty good shape for a mom. She looks almost like a teenager in her navy blue swimsuit.

Then Daddy picks her up and walks with her out into the water. Mom screams and kicks and acts like she's about to die, but she's laughing the whole time.

"Put me down, Sam!" she squeals.

"Your wish is my command!" Daddy says. Then he tosses Mom into the oncoming wave.

She screeches, goes under the wave, and comes up laughing and sputtering. She swims over to Daddy and pulls him under the water. The two of them look like kids as they play.

"Swim tag!" Sabin cries. He tags me first, and I tag

Sadora, who catches Mom. Mom tags Daddy, but I think he lets her catch him. Poppy is the fastest swimmer of all of us, so he never gets caught.

When the game is over, I lie on my back and just float and bobble on the waves. I look up at the blueness of the sky and at the crisp white clouds, and I almost want to cry because it's just so pretty.

Sadora swims over and floats like a lovely fish next to me. "Pretty nice, huh, Little Sister?"

"Awesome," I reply quietly.

"The water feels like a warm, soft bed," she says.

"Pretty wet and bouncy for a bed," I joke.

"It seems like that hurricane is a million miles from here," she says.

"And I hope it stays there," I tell her with feeling.

I float quietly, dreaming of birthday parties in the sunlight and campfires on the beach in the moonlight.

Then Sabin swims over to me, splashes water across my face, and I have to chase him again.

Mom and Daddy and Poppy finally get tired and head to the beach, but Sabin and Sadora and I stay in the warm water as long as we can.

I finally notice that Grammy is calling us in. She has blankets and towels spread out on the sand. I can see paper plates and napkins and cups. I can smell the food from here.

"Food!" Sabin says as we get closer. "I could eat a horse!"

"I'm starving!" Sadora says.

"Me, too!" I yell. We race one another to the blankets.

Mom and Grammy have brought out hot dogs and hamburgers and chips, along with a huge jug of lemonade and a large package of chocolate chip cookies.

"Why does food taste so much better when you eat it outside?" I ask as I eat my second hot dog.

"Must be a combination of wind and surf and fresh air," Poppy tells me with his mouth full.

"Mmm," Sabin mumbles. "We should do this all the time!"

We're slightly damp, and our legs and feet are covered with sand. We sit together on our own private spread, gobbling food, laughing, and watching the sun go down.

"The sun looks like a huge golden ball falling slowly in the sky," Sadora says.

"It seems like it should sizzle as it touches the water," I add with a giggle.

"The moon is already up and ready to take over." Sabin points at the dim disk in the sky.

"It looks like somebody took a bite out of it!" I tell him.

"Can we stay out until it gets dark and the moon and stars are bright?" I ask Mom and Grammy.

"You can stay out until the beach bugs chase you in,"

Poppy replies with a laugh. "Those little insects will cover your legs with little tiny bites."

This time it's Mom's turn to dig into her bag and pull out just what we need. "I brought bug spray and lotion for everyone," she announces.

"It stinks," Sadora complains as she spreads the lotion on her arms.

"Then don't use it," Grammy tells her. "But you'll be sorry!"

Sadora mumbles something about being first in the shower, but she rubs lots of the lotion on her feet and legs. I like the spray kind because I don't have to get it all over my hands.

The sun disappears gradually. "Seems like the earth just swallowed the sun," I say.

I shiver a little because it's gotten cooler.

"Too bad we don't have a fire," Sabin says.

"It would take too long to gather firewood," Poppy says. "Let's just pack up our stuff and head in."

"No, wait! I have an idea!" I tell my family. "I think I know how to start a fire." I dig down into my sack.

"What do you have in there that can make fire?" Sabin asks.

I'm digging and digging. Then my fingers touch what I'm looking for.

"This I gotta see," Sadora says, rolling her eyes.

I pull out two slightly flattened packages of corn chips. "Do you have a lighter, Poppy?" I ask.

"Sorry, Sassy. I don't."

"But I have some waterproof matches in *my* sack," Grammy says. "I believe in being prepared." She pulls them out of her bag and hands them to me.

Even though I can't see their faces very well in the moonlight, I know my entire family is curious. "Just wait and see," I tell them. "I learned this in science class."

I open the packages and push the corn chips into a little pile. Then I carefully strike one of the matches on its box. The spark burns blue, then red. Slowly, slowly, I touch the match to the corn chips, and amazingly, they light! We have a fire!

"Terrific!" Daddy says.

"Awesome!" Sadora adds.

"Out of sight!" Grammy says. Only Grammy or Poppy would say that.

"It's amazing what Sassy can find in that sack," Mom says proudly. "Simply amazing!"

"That's crazy!" Sabin says with real admiration in his voice. He adds a few sticks he finds nearby to the little fire.

Then Daddy and Poppy add a few more sticks and branches from the dunes.

The stars above are bright. The moon glows like a dim cookie in the distance. And my corn-chip fire burns brightly on the beach.

CHAPTER SIX

Beach Secrets and Surprises

I'm too excited to sleep, so the next morning I wake up really early. It's still dark outside. I leave Sadora snoring and tiptoe down the steps to Grammy's kitchen.

She sits at her kitchen table, sipping a cup of tea. Next to her is a steaming mug of hot chocolate.

"Good morning, Sassy," Grammy says with a smile. "I knew you'd be up with the birds." She slides the mug of chocolate over to me.

"Yum. Chocolate-raspberry, my favorite," I whisper as I sip. "Is Poppy still asleep?"

Grammy chuckles. "Your grandfather is pretty pooped. He tried to run and play like he was a teenager yesterday, but this morning his body is telling him he's not! He'll be sleeping late this morning."

"How long have you known Poppy?" I ask.

Grammy gazes out the window and smiles. "You've heard this story before, Sassy."

"I know. Tell me again. I love to hear it."

Grammy takes another sip of her tea and begins. "I was a teenager, not much older than Sadora. I went to the history museum with my school. I thought it would be just another boring look at dusty old relics. But our tour guide was a skinny college kid who *loved* old things and he made the whole trip seem like a great adventure. He told funny stories about cavemen and dinosaurs and ancient mummies. He knew juicy details about each exhibit. He made me laugh." She paused.

"So then what happened?" I ask.

"Well, every Saturday after that, I rode the bus to the museum so I could see that amazing young man and learn more about history. He and I got to be good friends. Years later, after we both finished college, we got married, and a few years after that, your mom was born."

"Great story," I tell her as I slurp the last of my chocolate.

"Would you like to take an early morning walk on the beach?" Grammy asks.

"Can we hunt for shells?" I ask.

"Of course!" Grammy says. "And the sunrise this morning should be beautiful."

I grab a jacket, my sandals, and my Sassy Sack, and we head out into the dawn. The sky is starting to get brighter and I can see the sun peeping at the ocean in the distance.

"Can I take my shoes off?" I ask Grammy.

"Oh, yes, let's do that!" Grammy says. She removes her sandals, too.

The sand feels cool and squishy under my toes. I take Grammy's hand.

"Are you excited about your birthday, Grammy?" I ask her.

She chuckles a little. "When you get to be my age, I'm just glad to *have* a birthday!" she replies. "But yes, I'm looking forward to the party."

I reach down and pick up two perfectly curled shells. I toss them into my sack. "Where do all the shells come from?" I ask Grammy.

"From deep within the sea," she tells me. "Shells are the crowns of the kings and queens of the ocean, and they send them to us as gifts to treasure. When the sun goes to sleep, she gathers all the shells, then tosses them on the beach at dawn for us to find."

"Is that one of your folktales, or is that for real?" I ask her.

"A little of both," she admits.

"You know so much, Grammy," I tell her. "I feel like I'll never figure everything out like you have."

"I've been blessed, Sassy. I've been given lots of time to learn. But there's still lots I don't know."

"Like what?"

"Like how to paint my toenails so the polish doesn't smear!"

I giggle. "That's easy! Just put cotton between your toes!"

"See, there's lots of stuff you know that I don't!" We both crack up.

The sky is pink now, with edges of gold. "The water looks like blue ink with white foam on the edges," I whisper to Grammy.

She squeezes my hand.

The sun gets brighter and higher in the distance. I have to take off my jacket.

"Good morning, sunshine," I say to the sky.

"We'd better enjoy the sun while we can," Grammy says, pointing to some dark clouds in the distance. "I don't think today will be as bright as yesterday. And tomorrow might be pretty dismal."

I try not to worry about the upcoming storm.

Grammy and I collect lots of pretty shells, and the ocean waves keep us company as we walk. The *whoosh, whoosh* of the water is much louder than it was the day before. The surf is surging high.

"The waves seem like they're angry today," I tell Grammy. "They're pounding the sand."

"That's the storm that's brewing," Grammy says. "Let's head back to the house."

"Okay. I've worked up an appetite," I tell her.

Then she stops walking. "Look, Sassy!" Grammy says with excitement in her voice.

"What is it?" I ask.

She kneels down in the sand next to a large rock. "It's a sea turtle nest," she says softly.

"Wow! How can you tell?"

"See the tracks the mother left?" Grammy points to a long path in the sand. It leads all the way back down to the sea.

"It looks like the track of one giant truck wheel," I say.

"She deposited her eggs here last night and covered them with sand," Grammy explains.

"When will she come back to check on her babies?"

"She lays her eggs, then swims away. She will never return," Grammy tells me.

"Oh, that's so sad!"

"Most of these nests are marked by the Marine Turtle Protection Program, but it looks like they missed this one," Grammy says as she rubs her hand over the dent in the sand where the eggs are hidden.

"What difference does it make?" I ask.

"Sea turtles are endangered animals," Grammy explains.

"Does that mean they are about to be extinct?" I ask.

"Lots of people are working so that does not happen," Grammy tells me.

"How?"

"Well, the nests are usually marked so beachgoers know to be very careful. We want the little eggs to hatch."

"How many eggs to do you think are waiting under the sand?"

"Probably about a hundred," Grammy tells me.

"Wow."

I reach down into my Sassy Sack and pull out a bright green ribbon. Then I take my lucky pink ribbon from my hair.

"Can we tie these to a stick as a warning?" I ask.

"Great idea, Sassy," Grammy replies. "Are you sure you want to use your special pink ribbon?"

"If it's lucky for me, then maybe it will be good for the sea turtles," I tell her. I feel very sure of this.

We find a piece of driftwood and stick it deep into the sand near the big rock. Then I tie the ribbons to it. "Will this help?" I ask.

"Absolutely!" Grammy replies. "Whoever comes close will know that something special is hidden at that spot."

The wind blows a little harder at that moment. The ribbons flutter in the new breeze.

"Will the turtle eggs be okay?" I ask as we turn to leave.

"I hope so," Grammy replies. But she doesn't sound sure.

"Have you ever been in a hurricane?" I ask as we head back to the house.

"Yes. Once," Grammy replies. "It was pretty scary."

I shiver and grab her hand again. I am about to ask her to tell me about that storm, but Sabin is running down the beach toward us.

"Hey, there!" he cries out as he reaches us. "Where have you two been?"

"Just walking and talking," Grammy says.

I don't want to tell Sabin that I was glad I had a few minutes with Grammy all by myself.

"We found a sea turtle nest!" I announce proudly.

"Cool!" Sabin says. "Can you show it to me later?"

"Sure! We marked it with ribbons," I tell him.

"I'll race you back to the house!" Sabin says to me.

"What's your hurry?" Grammy asks.

"Because I'm hungry!" Sabin replies gleefully. "The sooner we get back, the sooner we can have breakfast!"

I crack up and run my fastest toward Grammy's house, but even in my bare feet on the sand, I'm no match for Sabin's long legs. He beats me down the beach and up the stone steps to the house. He waits on the deck as I catch up.

Grammy takes her time walking back. When she gets to her kitchen, she pops a pan of biscuits into the oven and starts a skillet of bacon sizzling on the stove. The whole house smells like yummy breakfast.

Sadora has taken the time to get dressed in a pair of shorts and a T-shirt. She has put on makeup and combed her hair. She walks into the kitchen, looking fresh and ready for the day.

"You look like a flower from Grammy's garden," I tell her.

"Is that good?" she asks.

"I guess so. At least you don't look like a weed!" We laugh and glance at Sabin.

"Who are you calling a weed?" he asks. His mouth is full of the peanut butter sandwich Grammy gave him so he would not starve before breakfast. "I might be skinny, but at least my hair doesn't explode!" He grins at me.

I glance into a mirror and I almost scream. My hair does not like damp ocean air. It is puffy and bushy and frizzy. And I don't have any hair gel.

"I look like a dandelion!" I yell.

Grammy looks up from slicing bananas for fruit salad.

"Relax, Sassy. You're on vacation. I'll help you fix your hair a little later."

Daddy and Mom come into the kitchen. Mom kisses Grammy on the cheek. "Can I help you with anything?" she asks.

"Breakfast is ready," Grammy announces. "Let's eat!"

Poppy enters the kitchen just as she says the food is ready. He's a lot like Sabin. "I'm starving!" he says in his booming voice.

"Grab a biscuit and grab a chair," Grammy tells him cheerfully.

"Can we talk about the party now?" Sabin asks after he finishes two plates of eggs and grits and fruit.

Grammy looks pleased. "The people who are bringing the food to the party called me this morning," she tells us. "They will deliver it Thursday morning. I think we have enough to feed a small army."

"You're not cooking?" Sabin asks as he eats another biscuit thick with butter and jelly.

"Goodness, no," Grammy says. "It's my birthday! Besides, I don't think I can cook enough to fill up both you and Poppy, Sabin!"

"What about the cake?" Sadora asks.

"The bakery called yesterday, and the cake will be delivered on Thursday also."

"How big is it?" Sabin wants to know.

"Huge!" Grammy tells him. "It might take you all day to finish it!"

"Chocolate?" Sabin looks hopeful.

"Half is chocolate and half is vanilla," Grammy explains. "The icing is cherry."

"Ooh, yum!" I say.

"Will the band play oldies music, or cool songs we like?" Sadora asks.

Grammy laughs. "Since I'm the birthday girl, I get to pick the music. And I *love* the old jams!"

Poppy jumps up from his chair, grabs Grammy around the waist, and the two of them dance, old style, in the kitchen.

Sadora slumps into her chair with a laugh. "We're doomed, Sabin! Old-school music all night long!"

"I've got my iPod," Sabin says. "Maybe we can sneak in some *real* music later on."

"Let's hope so," Sadora says.

"You'll set everything up on your deck?" Daddy asks Grammy and Poppy.

"The band will need electricity for their amps and speakers," Poppy says, "so they will need to be on the deck."

"What about the food?" Sabin asks.

"Great question!" Poppy replies.

"You certainly do have a one-track mind!" Grammy tells them. "The food will be on the deck also, just so it is close to the kitchen. Everything else will spill onto the beach."

I look out of Grammy's huge picture window. The sun is hiding behind thin purple clouds. The sand looks gray instead of yellow. I shiver a little.

"What will we do if it rains?" I ask quietly. I don't want to think of anything worse.

"Has anybody checked on what's happening with the hurricane?" Mom asks.

Daddy looks at Poppy. They have been very quiet during most of our talk about the party. Finally, Daddy says, "The storm is getting closer, and getting stronger. It does not look good."

CHAPTER SEVEN
Getting Ready for the Storm

After breakfast we are glued to Poppy's big-screen television. The weather forecasters seem to love storms. Every five minutes they give updates on what might happen. Every station tries to outdo the other.

"The storm is heading this way!" one announcer says on Channel Three.

"Prepare for the worst," says the weatherman on Channel Five.

"Wind! Rain! Thunder! Lightning!" the Channel Seven weather lady reports.

The weather people draw circles and arrows on weather maps, pointing to where the storm might hit. All of them look extremely excited and happy. They look like they want to jump up and dance.

I don't feel like dancing. Grammy's party is going to be

messed up. How can we dance on the beach in a hurricane? Our whole family looks sad.

Grammy speaks first. "Today is Tuesday. The storm is due on Thursday. We need to prepare."

"But Thursday is your birthday!" I wail.

"There's still a chance it will turn and go back out to sea," Sadora says hopefully.

"Suppose it doesn't?" Sabin asks quietly.

"This house is really tough," Poppy says with confidence. "We had it built with storms in mind. It is made of stone."

"Stones don't blow in the wind?" I ask. I'm a little scared.

"The windows are made of glass," Sadora says as she looks at the huge picture window that faces the ocean.

"You're right, Sadora, but Grammy and Poppy have storm shutters on most of the windows. The others we can board up," Daddy reminds her.

Grammy looks brave and relaxed. "Our home has weathered many big storms. And one small hurricane!" She takes Poppy's hand into hers.

"How bad was it?" I ask.

"Oh, it was about *this* bad!" Grammy says as she reaches for me. I guess she can see I'm a little scared, because she tickles me until I can't stop laughing.

In spite of all my giggles, Sadora says seriously, "All the weather forecasters are saying this storm is a Category One." I can tell she is really hoping this one will go away.

"Storms can grow," Mom adds.

I wonder about the sea turtles. "Daddy, are sea turtles safe in a hurricane?"

He stops to think. "Probably so," he says slowly. "Except for nesting, they live in the ocean all their lives. So I guess they're used to riding the big waves."

"But what about the babies in the nests on the beach?" I ask.

"I have heard of storm surges washing away turtle nests," Daddy tells me honestly.

"Oh, no!" I exclaim. "Me and Grammy found a sea turtle nest on the beach! What will happen to the eggs if we have a big storm?"

"If the storm is really big, the baby turtles might not make it," Daddy admits.

"Can we do anything about it?" Sabin asks.

"Let's make some phone calls this afternoon," Daddy suggests, "and see if we can find some answers."

"I've got friends I can call in the marine science department at the university," Poppy adds.

"Great idea," Mom agrees. "Sabin, you can check on the Internet and see what you can find out."

"In the meantime," Grammy says, "I need some help."

"Just tell us what you need," Daddy offers.

Grammy smiles. "Sam, can you and Sabin and Poppy help me board up the windows? We keep wood in the garage, just in case."

"Of course!" Daddy tells her. "Sabin, let's get busy." Poppy stands and stretches.

"I'd rather check for sea turtle Web sites," Sabin replies, looking hopeful.

"You plan to eat dinner?" Grammy asks him, hands on her hips.

"Sure! Actually, I'm just about hungry for lunch!"

"Well, I'm only feeding carpenters this afternoon!"

"Gotcha." Sabin jumps up, puts on his sneakers, and heads out to the garage with Daddy and Poppy.

Mom says, "Sadora and Sassy, let's go to the supermarket and pick up a few items."

Grammy chuckles. "Everybody in town will be there, buying food and flashlights. Plan to stand in line awhile!"

I love shopping. It doesn't matter if it's for clothes or for groceries. I just like being in a store, looking for stuff.

I run upstairs to change my clothes. Mom brushes my hair and whips it into a puffball with a ponytail holder. I race Sadora to Grammy's car.

Instead of using the air conditioner, we roll down the windows. The slight breeze feels good on my face.

"The air feels thick," Sadora says.

"Like soup," I say, nodding my head.

"But the sky is blue again, and those clouds don't look so scary." Sadora looks up at the sky.

Grammy is right about the grocery store. Crowds of people are rushing around, throwing items in their metal carts. Long lines of shoppers wait to be checked out at the register.

"This is worse than the airport," I whisper to Sadora.

Mom, dressed in a pretty yellow sundress, looks like a sunflower on a summer day. She grabs a cart.

"Let's see what goodies we can find, girls. Everybody seems to have the same plan as we do."

Sadora offers, "I'll go find some bags of ice. How many should I get?"

"Two or three," Mom replies.

Sadora walks off, looking for the ice machine.

"Should we buy party stuff?" I ask Mom. "You know, like streamers and balloons?"

"Let's focus on food," Mom tells me. She tosses cans of green beans and corn into the cart, along with cans of tuna and salmon.

"Yuck! Boring!" I tell her. I add a couple of packs of cookies and a box of Frosted Flakes.

Mom doesn't make me put them back, so I add several bars of chocolate candy, some corn chips, and a box of microwave popcorn.

Mom puts the popcorn back on the shelf. "Suppose we lose electricity?" she asks me.

"Is that possible?" I ask.

"Absolutely!" Mom tells me.

Sadora returns empty-handed.

"Where's the ice?" I ask her.

"They're all sold out," she tells us. "One lady told me there is no ice left in the whole town."

"I'm not surprised," Mom says. "Let's see what else we can find, girls. Look for items that do not have to go in the refrigerator."

In the fruit section, Sadora chooses bananas and apples and plums. I like oranges, so I add a bag of those.

"Can we get some canned fruit, Mom?" I ask.

"Good idea, Sassy," she says as we head to that aisle. I toss canned pineapple and peaches into our cart. Sadora adds applesauce.

"Let's get some bottled water," Sadora suggests.

There are only a few cases left. "Wow! I've never seen so many empty shelves in a store," I tell them.

"Maybe these people know something we don't know," Sadora says.

"They watch the same weather stations we do," Mom replies. "They're just like us. They want to be ready."

"For what?" I ask.

"For whatever comes," she replies.

That's a scary answer.

"Should we buy flashlights and batteries?" Sadora asks as we pass by that section of the store.

"I'm sure Grammy and Poppy have those in the house," I tell her. But we get two flashlights and extra batteries anyway, just in case.

"Let's buy some candles and matches, also," Mom suggests.

We put boxes of juice drinks, crackers, chips, and peanut butter in the cart.

"Did we get everything we might need?" Mom asks.

"Toilet paper," I suggest.

Mom nods and I go to find two packages.

"Maybe the party won't be canceled," I say hopefully. "Then we won't need all this stuff."

"But maybe we'll all get blown away like in *The Wizard of Oz!*" Sadora teases.

I don't answer her. I keep thinking about the poor little sea turtle babies all alone on the beach. I wonder if they will get blown away.

The checkout line is very long.

"People are buying crazy things," I whisper to Sadora. "Look at that lady in aisle three. Her whole cart is full of diet soda!"

Sadora laughs. "I guess she really likes the stuff!"

"And look at the lady in aisle one," I say, nudging Sadora. Her cart is filled with toys. Red plastic balls. Dolls. Cars. Games.

"I bet she has a house full of little kids," Sadora says. "I guess she wants to keep them busy."

We pay for our purchases and head out into the parking lot. The sun has finally broken through the clouds and the day is crisp and clear.

I look at the sky and smile. "I think everything is gonna be fine, Mom!"

She loads the groceries into the back of Grammy's SUV.

"I certainly hope so, Sassy. But this just might be the calm before the storm."

When we get back to Grammy's house, things have changed. The storm shutters are pulled down. The huge picture window is covered with wood.

"Her house was so pretty. Now it looks like a stone barn," I tell Sadora sadly.

"It's just temporary, Sassy."

"I know, but it still makes me sad. And a little scared," I admit.

I can hear the sound of hammering. Sabin and Poppy and Daddy must be working hard. I like to hammer, too. Maybe they will let me help later on.

We take the groceries into the house. Inside, instead of the sunlight coming through the many windows, the rooms are dim and dark. Grammy has already turned on lights.

"What is the latest from the Weather Channel?" Sadora asks as she helps Grammy put the canned goods away in the cabinets.

"The storm is still churning in the ocean. It looks like it is heading straight for us," Grammy explains.

I shudder. "It looks like we're going to have a real adventure!" I'm trying to sound brave.

Grammy puts the cookies and the candy on a high shelf and the fruit on the counter, where it can be easily reached. I smile at her because I know why she is doing it.

"Do you think we should evacuate, Grammy?" Sadora asks as Mom walks into the kitchen with the last bag of groceries.

"Lots of Grammy's neighbors have left the area," Mom tells us.

But Grammy looks calm. "I talked to your dad and your grandfather while you were gone, and we agree that we will be safe here. Our house is very strong."

"What if the house blows away?" I ask. I'm still thinking of Dorothy and Toto and *The Wizard of Oz*.

Grammy smiles. "Trust me, Sassy."

Poppy and Sabin and Daddy come back inside, looking hot and sweaty.

"Can I help hammer later?" I ask Poppy. I know that Daddy will tell me to wait until I'm bigger, but Poppy will let me try.

"Sure, Sassy," Poppy tells me as he wipes the sweat from his forehead. "Maybe I'll show you how to hold a hammer and nail safely. There is one small window that you can cover."

Daddy winks at me. He understands.

"I worked hard, Grammy," Sabin says. "Can I eat now?"

Grammy pats him on his back. "Go take a shower, Sabin, and I'll fix you a feast!"

Sabin runs up the steps two at a time.

Grammy really does fix a great dinner. She cooks all the food that might spoil if the electricity is cut off. So we have baked chicken with sliced tomatoes, and roast beef and lettuce salad.

"And for dessert," Grammy announces, "I guess we have to eat all my leftover ice cream! If the power goes out, it will melt."

Sabin cheers the loudest.

"Is this ice cream for the party?" I ask as I have my third bowl of chocolate-raspberry.

"No, the bakery is bringing fresh-churned ice cream to go with the cake," Grammy replies. "So enjoy!"

After dinner, feeling full and safe for now, I snuggle next to Grammy on the sofa. "I'm worried about the turtle babies," I admit to her.

"I was wondering when you would ask about the turtle nest," she says. "I made a couple of phone calls this afternoon while you were at the store."

"What did you find out?" Sadora asks.

"Well, I talked to a really nice man from the university who also works for the National Save the Sea Turtle Foundation."

"I didn't know there was such a thing," Sabin says.

"We Florida folks try to take good care of our wildlife," Grammy explains. "We have several organizations set up to help the turtles."

"What did he say?" I ask Grammy.

"He is coming here first thing in the morning, and he's going to see what needs to be done about the nest. He's a little worried about what the storm might do to the turtle eggs."

"Can we go down to the beach with him, Grammy?" I ask. "I can show him where the nest is hidden."

"Absolutely!" Grammy replies.

When we finally get to bed, it feels stuffy because the windows are boarded over. It is a long time before I fall asleep.

CHAPTER EIGHT

Turtle Rescue Mission

When I get up on Wednesday morning, I run downstairs and outside to see what the sky looks like. The dawn is thick and gray and cloudy. The ocean is dark, dark blue, and the edges look like whipped cream.

Grammy has come out on the deck with me. The wind whips her long orange dress. "Good morning, Sassy," she says.

"The hurricane is coming, isn't it, Grammy?" I ask.

"Yes, little one, it's coming," she replies. She puts her hand on my shoulder.

"What about your party?" I ask. "Tomorrow is your birthday!"

"I figure this will be one birthday I'll never forget!" she replies with a chuckle.

"I would hate it if my birthday got messed up," I tell her honestly.

Sadora and Sabin join us on the deck. They are both quiet while strong gusts of wind whip around us.

"The storm is like a monster in one of my video games," Sabin says finally. "Sometimes it's not on the screen, but you know it's there. You can feel it coming."

Sadora nods in agreement. "Is that why they give hurricanes names, Grammy? Because they are like real beings?"

"I suppose so," Grammy replies. "I can feel it, too. So can the birds and the squirrels. Even dogs and cats go and hide under their owners' beds."

"It's a funny sort of exciting feeling," I tell them. "Like just before you go down the hill on a roller coaster."

"Or just before you dive off the high board at the pool," Sadora adds.

"Or just before you jump out of an airplane!" Sabin says.

"What?" we all say together.

"Just kidding," Sabin says. "But I will do that one day."

"Don't forget your parachute," I remind him.

We laugh as we go back inside.

While we eat breakfast, Sabin tells us what he has learned from his Web search about sea turtles.

"Did you know that green sea turtles can weigh as much as three hundred fifty pounds?"

"For real?" I'm amazed.

"That's a lot of turtle soup!" he jokes.

I throw my sausage at him. "Yuck! Don't even *joke* like that!"

"Seriously," he continues, "they're really cool creatures, but they're endangered."

"But they won't become extinct, will they?" I ask. This worries me.

"As long as folks help them like we are doing," Daddy replies, "they have a chance."

Daddy puts another biscuit on Sabin's plate. I think he is real proud of Sabin for finding out all this science information.

"The poor little turtles are running out of beaches and places to lay their eggs," Sabin says.

"How come?" Sadora asks.

"Too many hotels and houses and restaurants on the beaches. Too many people," Poppy says, joining in.

"Turtles need space and silence, and people are taking it all away," Sabin adds sadly.

"Somehow we have to find a balance." Daddy frowns as he stirs his coffee. "It's a huge problem."

"You know that plastic bag that the lady at the airport wanted you to have, Sassy?" Sabin asks me.

"Yeah."

"Well, lots of sea turtles are dying because they eat the bags that are thrown away in the water."

"Why would they eat plastic bags?" Sadora asks.

"The bags float on the water and look like jellyfish," Poppy explains. "For sea turtles, jellyfish is like pizza to you."

"That's awful," I tell them.

Daddy nods. "Did you find out about how the females lay their eggs on the beach?" he asks Sabin.

"No, I got sleepy when I got to that part, and I shut the computer off," Sabin admits. "You're not gonna give me a science quiz, are you?"

We're laughing in the boarded-up living room when the doorbell rings.

Poppy goes to answer the door and invites the guest in. "This is my friend Michael," he announces. "He works with me at the university, and he's also active with the National Save the Sea Turtle Foundation."

"Wow," I whisper to myself. "Sea turtles have their own club!"

Michael looks like he spends every single day on the beach. His hair is bleached almost white and his skin is deeply tanned. He wears dark shorts, sandals, and a white T-shirt.

He grins at me. "You must be Sassy!" he says. He shakes my hand firmly.

"That's me!" I reply.

"Your grandfather told me how you and your grandmother found the sea turtle nest. We are so glad you called us."

"Because of the hurricane?" Sadora asks.

"Exactly," Michael replies. "We don't have much time, so who's going to help me?"

All of us raise our hands.

"Great. Go put on some clothes you can get dirty. We're going to be digging for the next couple of hours."

"Dirty?" Sadora makes a face, but she hurries upstairs with me to get changed.

Mom and Daddy, as well as Grammy and Poppy, decide to go with us down to the beach. Grammy carries two plastic buckets. In each bucket are three large serving spoons from her kitchen.

Mom carries four shovels from Poppy's garage, and Daddy totes a case of bottled water. Michael carries his own shovel and tools. Poppy brings a basket of snacks from the cupboard. I carry my Sassy Sack.

Michael walks very fast. It's hard to keep up with him. He seems to be very serious about what he is doing.

We get to the big rock. I can see, fluttering in the wind, the special pink ribbon I left yesterday. The green one is still there, too.

"There's the place," I tell Michael proudly.

He kneels down and examines the nest. The winds are increasing and sand blows in our faces.

"Where did you see the mother turtle track to the sea?" he asks me.

I point to where the turtle left her trail from the nest. The wind had blown so hard all night that the track was gone.

"She left her eggs too close to the shore," Michael announces.

"Why would she do that?" Sabin asks.

"Lights sometimes frighten turtles who are nesting. Or maybe she could feel that the hurricane was coming. She hurried to lay her eggs before she found a really safe place," Michael explains.

"So what will happen to the eggs?" Sadora asks. Her hair is blowing in the wind.

"Unless we move them," Michael says, "the storm surge will wash them all away."

"Move them?" I ask.

"Yep!" Michael answers cheerfully. "We're going to dig up some turtle eggs and move them to a safer place."

"Are folks allowed to dig up sea turtle eggs whenever they feel like it?" Sadora asks, frowning.

"Good question," Michael answers. "And the answer is absolutely not! I'm employed by the University of Florida and I'm trained in conservation and rescue skills. The ordinary person who is caught digging up sea turtle eggs would go to jail."

"He's right," Daddy adds.

"Where will we move the eggs?" Sabin asks.

Michael points to an area about two hundred feet away. It is in the sand dunes, way above the highest point the tide reaches.

"Up there by the sea oats?" Poppy asks.

Michael nods and heads in that direction.

"What are sea oats?" I ask. "Not a breakfast food, right?

Michael laughs. "Actually, sea oat seeds, when they are dried and cooked, make a pretty good cereal with honey and skim milk!"

"Not for me," Sabin says.

"I've seen sea oats in really pretty floral decorations," Sadora says. "They remind me of the wind blowing on the beach."

"Let's get started," Daddy says. "The wind is increasing. We must hurry."

Daddy passes out serving spoons to the children and shovels to the grown-ups.

Michael explains. "We must be very careful. When we find the nest, Sabin and Sassy are to dig out the eggs. Sadora, you must keep them packed in sand."

"How come?" she asks.

"That's what keeps them warm and alive," Daddy explains.

We dig carefully for a few minutes, then again a few inches away. I get all sweaty, even though the wind is blowing pretty hard.

Then Michael says, "I think those spoons you're using are too big, kids. I wish we had something smaller. We need to be *really* gentle."

"I think I have just the right thing," I say with excitement. I dig down into my Sassy Sack and pull out three plastic spoons from the school cafeteria. "Will these work?"

Michael looks pleased. "Perfect, Sassy," he says. "Now, carefully, gently, let's find and remove the eggs."

Finally, Sadora calls out with excitement, "I see an egg, I think. I found the nest!"

Poppy plops down on the sand with us and uses his hands and fingers to carefully uncover the amazing pile of eggs. "Gently, gently," he says.

"Have you ever done this before, Poppy?" I ask.

"You mean search for eggs and move them to safety before a hurricane?" He wipes his brow. Sand and dirt cover his face and hair, but his eyes twinkle at me.

I figure Poppy probably knows and has done everything there is to know and do.

"Nope!" he replies with a grin. "This is the very first time I've saved sea turtles. I'm glad I get to save them with you, Sassy."

As he pushes more sand away from the eggs, it becomes clear that we have found a very large nest.

"They look like soft, dirty Ping-Pong balls!" I exclaim. I'm not afraid to touch them, which surprises me.

Michael looks in his pocket. "Oh, no! I left my notebook in my truck. I need to record what we are doing and count the eggs."

I scoop down in my Sassy Sack and pull out a small note-book and a well-used yellow pencil. "Will this help?" I ask.

"Perfect, Sassy!" Michael says. He looks pleased. He begins to scribble notes and draw pictures of the eggs and the nest.

I feel proud that I can help.

"I wish I had my camera with me," Daddy says. "I'd love to have pictures to show to my science students next year." He frowns as he digs.

I reach down into my Sassy Sack and pull out a small throwaway camera. "Here, Daddy," I say.

Daddy's frown turns into a smile. "I can always count on you, Little Sister! Thanks!"

He drops his shovel and snaps lots of photos of the turtle eggs and nest.

Carefully, Sabin and I scoop the eggs out of the warm sand and into the waiting buckets. We move them one at a time.

"Don't drop them!" I warn him.

"I've got this," he says. "You just watch what you're doing!"

He sounds fussy, but I can tell he's having a good time. He's forgotten his iPod, and he hasn't asked for food in an hour. Daddy snaps a picture of Sabin's serious, concentrating face.

Sadora packs the eggs carefully in more sand. "I'm getting sand in my fingernails," she complains.

Mom tells her, "Why don't you and I go get a manicure when the storm is over?"

Sadora looks happy when she hears this.

"Can I go, too?" I ask. "My nails are dirtier than hers!"

"Sure, Sassy," Mom says. "But first let's get this job done."

I try to count the eggs as we take them out of their hiding place and move them to the buckets. I'm pretty sure there are eighty-seven.

"One turtle laid all these eggs?" I ask Michael.

"Yep!" He grins at me. He takes more notes.

"That's crazy!" I reply.

Finally, all the eggs have been removed from the nest near the waves. All that's left is a hole in the sand. I double-check to make sure we have found every single egg.

Poppy, still on his hands and knees, helps me to check.

"You did a great job, Sassy," he whispers to me.

We both sit on the beach, gazing at the water, and brush the sand off our hands. I can feel the sea breeze on my face.

Daddy and Mom sit close to each other on the sand. Sabin and Sadora sit near Grammy.

"I think this is the first time I've ever *worked* at the beach," Sabin says, shaking his head. "Usually I just play."

"And I *never* get dirty!" Sadora admits with a laugh. "Never!"

Michael marches over to where our family sits, tired and dirty. He looks very proud of us. "Good work," he says, "but we're only halfway done."

"Is it time to move them to their new home, Michael?" I ask.

"Yep!" he says. "Let's move them, troops!" He sounds like a soldier.

"How do we know we're putting them in the right place?" Sadora asks with worry in her voice. She stands and brushes some of the sand off her shorts.

"And how do we know we didn't hurt them by touching them and moving them?" Sabin wants to know.

"First of all, we were *very* careful, and I'm a sea turtle expert. I promise the little eggs will be safe from the storm."

"Will they hatch?" I ask.

"Now, that I can't promise, but I'm pretty sure they won't notice they've been moved, and when it's time for them to hatch, they'll pop out and head back to the sea."

"How do the babies know to head toward the ocean?" I ask.

Daddy answers in his "science teacher" voice. "As soon as the hatchlings squirm out of their shells, which is usually at night, they start crawling toward the brightest light. Because of the moon and the stars, the ocean is usually the brightest thing that the babies see."

"Except we have built so many hotels with bright lights near the beaches, that the little turtles often get confused," Michael adds. "They crawl to the hotel lights instead of the ocean."

"Then what happens?" Sabin asks.

"They don't survive. They need the sea to live," Michael answers softly.

Everybody is quiet as we march up toward the top of the sand dune.

Daddy and Poppy dig another hole in the same shape and size as the first one, then we carefully put all the eggs back.

"Just a few at a time," Michael warns. "We have to cover them with sand the same way the mother turtle did."

One by one we carefully lift the eggs from the buckets and back to the new hole in the sand.

I whisper a message to each egg just before I place it in the new nest. "Swim strong, little one," I tell it. "The ocean is straight ahead. Watch out for hotel signs," I tell another one. "There is danger there."

Sadora is filthy dirty and never looked happier. Sabin's face is serious as he transfers the eggs from the buckets to the sand. Mom is sweaty and cracking jokes. Daddy snaps pictures. Poppy's curly gray hair is thick with sand. Grammy stands on a dune, the wind blowing her clothes around her. She is smiling at the whole scene.

When the last eggs are placed, Michael smooths the sand around the new nest.

"Great job, troops!" He salutes us like an army captain. We salute back.

"Can I leave my ribbons here so we can find the new nest?" I ask.

"Good idea, Sassy," Grammy says. She helps me tie the ribbons on a stick. Then we tuck the bottom of the ribbons under a rock so they will not fly away. The lucky pink one seems to flutter proudly.

"Did we save the turtles, Michael?" I ask.

"Yes, Sassy. Because of you and your family, those sea

turtles will hatch in a few weeks and return to the ocean. They will live!"

I feel so proud. Then a sudden gust of wind almost blows me over.

Mom says, "We'd better get back to the house."

"Leave no plastic on the beach," Michael reminds us. "Gather up your water bottles and any other trash you might see."

We gather our stuff and hurry back to Grammy and Poppy's house.

"Would you like to stay for dinner, Michael?" she asks him.

"No, thank you, ma'am," he replies. "I have two small children at home who need their daddy during a hurricane."

"We understand. Drive carefully, and thanks so much for your help!" Grammy says.

Poppy and Michael shake hands and talk for a few minutes, then Michael hurries to his truck and drives away. Even though it is still early afternoon, the sky is almost as dark as nighttime.

We stand in the driveway, waving good-bye. The palm trees sway and bend with each strong gust of wind.

I look at my family and crack up. "We look like a dirty

mess!" I say, pointing at them. "But we did a great thing today."

"I've got dibs on the big bathroom!" Sabin cries out.

I run to the front door, but he beats me, as usual. Sadora runs to the little bathroom. I don't mind waiting.

The wind is blowing really hard. The storm is very close. And eighty-seven sea turtles are sleeping safely tonight.

CHAPTER NINE

The Hurricane

Thursday morning is dark and dreary. It's raining hard and the wind whistles as it blows outside. The rain sounds angry, like it's pounding and punching at everything in its way. The house shakes a little.

All of us are huddled in the middle of Grammy's living room floor. We have slept all night in sleeping bags with pillows from the bedrooms. They feel soft and comforting.

"Is it morning yet?" I ask Mom as I wake up. "It's so dark outside I can't tell."

"Yes, Sassy, it is," Mom answers quietly.

Poppy wakes up and turns over on his big blue pillow. He sits up and stretches. "Great night for a campout, folks! Great day for a birthday!" He leans over and kisses Grammy on the cheek. She smiles like a teenager.

I get up and cross over everybody's pillow and sleeping bag to get to Grammy. I plop down on her lap. "Happy birthday, Grammy," I say quietly.

She hugs me and holds me for a long time. "Thanks, Sassy."

Sabin and Sadora wish her a great birthday also. So do Mom and Daddy.

"What about the party?" I ask.

Lightning flashes. Thunder rolls in the distance.

"I called everyone last night and canceled," Grammy explains. She does not sound sad.

"The whole town is shut down anyway," Daddy tells me. "The bakery is closed. The caterer is at home with her own family. The band is packed away and safe."

"Nothing is open?" Sabin asks.

"No stores. No banks. No restaurants," Daddy answers.

"What about the police and fire station?" Sadora wants to know.

"I'm sure they are working extra hard to make sure everyone is safe," Daddy replies.

"The wind sounds like howling wolves," I whisper to Grammy.

"I've never actually heard a wolf howl," Grammy says, "but I'm sure this is the sound they make."

"In the story of 'The Three Little Pigs,' the Big Bad Wolf huffs and puffs until he blows their houses down," I remind her.

"Don't forget," Grammy tells me, "the house of the third little pig stands strong and does *not* get blown away."

"Because it is made of brick and stone?" Sabin asks.

"Just like our house," Poppy says.

"I think I feel a little better," I tell Sadora.

"But we're not pigs, and this is not a storybook," Sabin teases. I throw a pillow at him.

We still have electricity for now. The lights in the living room look dim, and sometimes they flicker.

For some reason we all speak in whispers and walk real slow when we get up, like we are tiptoeing in deep grass. Even Sabin is unusually quiet.

"Can I have a candy bar?" he asks.

Instead of a lecture on good health, Mom just gives him the candy.

"This is amazing!" I tell Sadora.

Daddy turns the TV on. All the television stations are showing only weather reports and commercials.

"Look at the weatherman," Daddy says with a chuckle. "He has taken off his jacket and tie."

The reporter looks like he has not slept. He talks about swirls and wind gusts. "The hurricane has grown to a Category Two!" he announces with excitement.

Grammy's front door has a thick safety-glass window. It is the only one not boarded up, so I stand there and watch in amazement.

Dirt swirls and mixes with the downpour. "It's raining mud!" I cry out.

Sabin and Sadora join me. We watch the hurricane happen.

"The palm trees look like ballet dancers, bending in the wind," Sadora says.

"The tops of the trees look like flags flapping," I add.

"Look at those birds!" Sabin cries. He points at the dark sky. "They're flying backward!"

The birds are flapping their wings as hard as they can, but the wind is pushing them back. I feel sorry for them.

"Where do you think birds hide in a storm like this?" I wonder out loud.

"Trees sure are not a good idea," Sadora says.

The rain pours and roars. It pounds the house. It blows sideways and in circles. We can only see a few feet in front of us because the heavy rain covers everything like a giant wet blanket that is blowing in the storm.

And the wind. It howls and growls. It screeches and shrieks. It snarls like a huge beast. It is easy to think the Big Bad Wolf is out there, trying to blow our house down.

We watch a huge tree in Grammy's yard bend, then twist, then fall with a thud. I jump.

"Get away from that door," Mom warns. The three of us do what she says right away.

"Can we peek out of the back window?" Sabin asks. "I wonder what the water looks like."

"Look!" Sadora says. "If you peek through right here where the boards are not nailed close together, you can see the ocean."

We run to the back and take turns looking down at the sea through the small opening. It looks angry. Huge waves batter the beach.

"The waves look taller than Daddy," I whisper.

"And angrier than when I don't put his tools back," Sabin replies.

"Would you like to be down there on the beach right now?" Sadora asks me.

"No way!" I tell her. "I'd be like a leaf on a tree — tossed far, far away."

"Do you think the sea turtles are okay?" Sabin asks.

"I sure hope so," I tell him with feeling.

Lightning crackles and the sky burns bright for a second. The loudest thunderclap in the universe booms right after that. The noise makes me shudder.

The wind blows stronger. It whirls around the house like an angry monster. It seems like it will never stop roaring and swirling and stomping. The rain beating on the sturdy little house sounds like a drum.

Suddenly, without warning, the lights flicker and go out. It is very dark.

CHAPTER TEN

A Hurricane Birthday Party

When the lights go out, I scream and squeeze myself tightly between Grammy and Poppy. Sadora runs to Mom. Sabin is not ashamed to run to Daddy. It's scary.

Daddy clicks on a flashlight. Mom lights a couple of candles.

"What do we do?" I whisper.

"Listen!" Grammy says.

The wind howls and blows. The rain thuds and thumps.

"All I can hear is hurricane!" Sabin cries.

"No, really, really listen," Grammy insists. "Do you hear the music of the storm?"

"Huh?" Sabin answers.

"Sh-sh-sh," Grammy whispers.

I close my eyes. "I can hear a deep moaning sound," I say softly. "Like the world is singing a sad song."

"It sounds like the deep bass drums in the orchestra," Sabin says.

"Maybe what we hear are ghosts," Sadora says. "A thousand dancing ghosts."

Grammy says, "Nothing is really scary if you make up stories about it. This storm is a powerful story. Nothing more."

I'm not so scared now. Grammy hugs me tightly as we listen to the whirling, swirling storm around us.

We sit in the darkness. The candles flicker. The storm pounds Poppy and Grammy's house, but it is safe and strong just like the third little pig's house.

"We need to do something silly and fun," Daddy says. "Let's sing a song." Then Daddy starts to sing in the dark silence. He has a strong bass voice. Mom joins in with her pretty soprano. Poppy can't sing at all. He tries, but it doesn't sound like music when he sings. His voice sounds a little like the noise that comes from a sick bird. Grammy rolls her eyes and lets him sing anyway. Soon we all join in.

The ants go marching one by one, hurrah, hurrah
The ants go marching one by one, hurrah, hurrah
The ants go marching one by one
The little one stops to suck his thumb
And they all go marching down to the ground
To get out of the rain, BOOM! BOOM! BOOM!

We take the ants through three, four, five, and six. By the time we get to the ants marching by nine and ten, we are all giggling and feeling better.

The ants go marching ten by ten, hurrah, hurrah
The ants go marching ten by ten, hurrah, hurrah
The ants go marching ten by ten
The little one stops to say "THE END"
And they all go marching down to the ground
To get out of the rain, BOOM! BOOM! BOOM!

When we finish the song, everybody is laughing. The rain is still falling, but it's no longer pounding the house quite so hard. The wind seems to be blowing slower. The moaning sounds more like a whisper.

"Is the storm over, Daddy?" I ask.

"I think this is what they call the *eye* of the storm, Sassy," Daddy explains. "The winds blow in a circle around a clear, calm center. That center will pass over us, then we'll get the other half of the storm."

"More wind and rain?" Sadora asks with a sigh.

Poppy tells us, "Surrounding the eye is the eyewall. That's a huge ring of thunderstorms with the strongest winds in the hurricane. So we've got a little calm, then a big surge, then the rest of the storm will hit us."

"It will probably rain even harder soon, with heavy winds all day and all night," Mom says.

"It might be worse than the first part," Grammy warns.

"I'm glad we're all together," Sadora admits.

Just as Daddy and Poppy had said, the winds begin to increase. The rain pounds harder than before. The winds whistle louder.

"It sounds like hundreds of furious whirling wind monsters out there," I whisper.

"Angry, wet ghosts," Sadora adds.

"Angry, wet ghosts with an attitude!" Sabin says, almost laughing.

The house seems to shudder in the storm. I can hear thumping noises outside, like things falling or knocking around.

"What are those noises?" Sadora asks.

"Trees falling, perhaps," Poppy replies.

"Or flying lawn furniture," Grammy tells us. "Sometimes, the day after a storm, we find things that have flown a long distance."

"Remember we found that mailbox from Georgia a couple of years back?" Poppy asks Grammy.

"Yes, it had flown off its pole and somehow landed in our yard. It still had mail inside."

"Amazing," Sabin says. "Did you find the owners of the mailbox?"

Grammy chuckles. "They told us we could keep the mailbox, and we mailed their letters back to Georgia. We still get Christmas cards from them!"

Suddenly, a huge gust of wind blasts the house. I tremble. We can hear something breaking and cracking outside. I try not to cry out, but it's really scary. I huddle closer to Grammy and Poppy.

"Are you sure we shouldn't have left town?" Sadora asks as another huge gust attacks the house.

"Well, it's too late to leave now, but we're pretty sure of the strength of the house," Poppy answers. "There's no way I'd let my children and grandchildren be in danger!"

The storm continues to rage outside, but inside we are warm and dry. I feel very safe, even though it's very dark. The candles flicker like little signals of hope.

"Will the lights come back on soon, Grammy?" I ask her. I'm trying not to fall asleep.

"Maybe not for a couple of days, Sassy. But we'll be just fine," Grammy tells me.

Daddy lights a few more candles. They smell like strawberries as they burn.

"Can we eat in the dark, Grammy?" Sabin asks.

Everybody laughs.

Sadora takes a candle to the kitchen and makes a huge pile of peanut butter sandwiches. Mom slices fruit. I get juice boxes for everyone and Daddy serves potato chips in a bowl.

"I'm glad we have some junk food," I tell Sadora. "Otherwise we would be eating cold green beans from a can!"

"Well, it looks like we're going to have a birthday party after all," Grammy announces when everyone is settled.

"We can't have a party," I wail.

"Why not?" Mom asks.

"We don't have a cake!"

"And we don't have a band!" Sabin says.

"And we don't have any decorations," I add.

"Is that what makes a birthday?" Grammy asks us.

I wrinkle up my face. "I wanted your party to be special, Grammy."

"It could not be any better," she replies.

"But you don't even have any power!" Sabin complains. "I bought you two CDs. But you can't play them."

Sadora nods in agreement. "I bought you an electronic picture frame, but we have no electricity!"

Grammy looks at both of them. "Those things will work in time. The electricity will come back. And I will love those gifts."

Mom looks at Daddy in the candlelight. They act like they understand what Grammy means.

"How can we have a party without all the party stuff?" I ask again.

Grammy smiles at me. "I have my family here. We are all safe in this storm. What a great party!"

I think I see what she means.

I ask Daddy, "Can I use one of the flashlights?" The circle of light looks odd on the dark wall as I go up the steps.

I go to our bedroom, and I find my Sassy Sack. I unzip one of the inside pockets and pull out a small item wrapped in silver paper. It's a little lumpy. I'm glad the lady at the security line did not find this one.

Slowly, I walk back down the stairs. Wind still swirls around the house.

"Happy birthday, Grammy," I say as I hand her the package. "I made this myself."

Grammy hugs me. "Thank you, Sassy. Hold the flashlight so I can see it."

She carefully unwraps the package. I hope she likes it.

"It's lovely!" Grammy says. She holds it up for everyone to see. "A bracelet made of seashells."

"Every time we visit, I look for the perfect shell," I tell her. "Mom helped me put them on the chain."

Grammy puts the bracelet on and smiles at me. The pink shells tinkle as they bump together.

And the wind seems to be quieter outside. Maybe the worst of the storm is over.

"Well, let's sing 'Happy Birthday'!" Poppy says. "It's not a party unless we sing that song!"

"Everybody join hands!" Mom suggests.

Sabin takes Sadora's hand, and she joins hands with Mom, who holds Daddy's hand. I hold Grammy's hand on one side and Poppy's hand on the other.

We stand in a small circle in the living room. Candles flicker. Flashlights shine. Nobody pays much attention to the storm.

Mom's soprano starts the song and I sing with her. We begin the song. Daddy's bass joins in, then Sadora's alto and Sabin's tenor. Even Poppy's sick-bird voice sounds good.

Happy birthday to you!
Happy birthday to you!
Happy birthday, dear Grammy!
Happy birthday to you!

What a wonderful birthday party!

CHAPTER ELEVEN

After the Storm

"**I**s it over?" I ask as soon as I wake up. I sit up, rub my eyes, and take a deep breath. I don't even remember falling asleep.

"Is it still raining?" asks Sadora, who had slept next to me on the pillows.

"The storm is over. The sun is out," Mom tells us. "And we are safe." She sounds relieved.

"Can we go outside, Dad?" Sabin asks.

"Yes, we can do that after breakfast," Daddy tells him.

"I feel like we are on a campout," Sabin says. "It's fun sleeping on pillows in the living room."

"Is the electricity back on?" Sadora asks. "I really need to fix my hair."

"Sorry, no power yet," Grammy replies. "And your hair looks fine." She hands Sadora a brush and a comb.

I can see sunshine peeking through the boarded-up windows. I go to the back window, where I can see a little bit of the ocean. Today the water no longer looks like a raging lion about to attack. It now looks like a kitten, lapping milk from a saucer. It is blue and calm once again.

The beach, however, looks pretty bad. It seems to be covered with branches and sticks and lots of yucky foamy stuff.

After a breakfast of fresh fruit and granola bars, we head outside to see what the storm did overnight.

When we open the front door, the sun is bright and cheerful in a clear, blue sky. Fluffy white clouds look like they have been painted up there. The air is moist and wet.

But Grammy's yard is a mess. Leaves and branches and all kinds of plants are broken and thrown around. I can see a lawn chair, a garbage can, and a large piece of jagged wood.

Three trees are completely down. Two are lying on the ground with their roots showing. The other one is broken in half.

"I have never seen anything like this," I whisper to Sadora.

We walk carefully over the debris.

"That tree is blocking the driveway," Sabin says.

"It looks like we'll have to get out the chain saw," Daddy says.

"Can I help?" Sabin asks. He looks excited.

"Sure," Daddy replies. "It looks like you'll get lots of practice today."

"Me, too?" I ask.

"I'm sure there will be some hammering and fixing you can do, Sassy," Poppy replies. "I promised to teach you, remember? But let's leave the chainsawing to Sabin and your dad, okay?"

"Sounds like a plan," I tell Poppy.

"What about your neighbors, Grammy?" Sadora asks.

"Most of them left town for high ground or a safer place," Grammy replies.

Mom says, "I hope their homes are not damaged."

"We'll go check on them this afternoon," Grammy tells us. "Some will need food and help when they return."

Mom gives me a broom and I start to sweep the bits and pieces scattered around Grammy's yard into piles. Mostly, I clean up branches and leaves and blown sand. But I also find amazing things — some big, some small.

One perfect conch shell — unbroken. A gold watch — still ticking. Half of a ticket to Disney World. A baseball. A bottle of Ruby Red nail polish. Three plastic bracelets. A Barbie doll, dressed for a party with her shoes still on.

"Where do you think these things came from?" I ask Grammy.

"The wind is quite powerful and sometimes things get blown very long distances," she tells me.

"Did any of your stuff get blown away?" Sadora asks Grammy.

"My flowers look like they lost a fistfight," Grammy replies with a laugh.

"And we lost a few trees," Poppy adds. "But I think everything else is still here."

Sadora and I line up all the unbroken items neatly on Grammy's porch.

"I hope that the little girl who owns this Barbie can find her," I tell her.

She nods. "And I'm sure the person who lost the watch needs to know what time it is."

I look at Grammy's yard and gaze beyond to the road, where bent trees and debris have been tossed everywhere. "Nothing is the same, is it?" I ask her.

"It's the same, but changed somehow," she says, agreeing with me. "Like a page has been torn out of a book and you can't find the same words again."

"Deep," I whisper.

"Were you scared?" she asks me.

"A little. If I had been by myself, I would have been crazy-scared. But I had my family with me, so I felt safe."

"I hope everybody else in the area is okay," Sadora says.

"Me, too. Can we go to the beach now?" I ask Daddy when we finish sweeping. "I'm worried about the sea turtle eggs."

"Good idea, Sassy," Daddy says.

"I was just getting the hang of the chain saw!" Sabin boasts.

Daddy winks at me. "We can take a break from the saw for a while, Sabin. Let's check for any beach damage."

All of us carefully take the stone steps down to the beach. Daddy and Sabin go first, then Grammy and Sadora, then me and Poppy and Mom. It's very slow going because the steps are wet and covered with sand.

"I can sweep these steps later," Sadora offers.

"Thanks, Sadora," Grammy replies, giving her a hug.

The beach is covered with seaweed and branches and sea foam. It looks sad. Lots of plastic bottles and soda cans also litter the area. A few dead fish make the sand smell funny.

"Look at this!" I say with amazement. "It's like a different beach."

"Will it ever be clean and pretty again?" Sadora asks with concern.

"The tides will wash all of this away in a few days," Grammy tells us. "And those of us who live near the beach must help to clean it up as well."

"Nature has a way of cleaning up," Daddy explains. "But we can help by getting all the bottles and junk."

"People shouldn't throw stuff on the beaches and in the ocean anyway," Sabin says angrily.

"You're right," Mom tells him.

"Where is all the sand?" Sadora asks as she gazes into the distance. "Everything looks sort of naked and bare."

"Hurricanes cause lots of beach erosion," Poppy explains. "The sand gets sucked into the storm surge and back out to sea."

"Will the sand come back?" Sabin asks.

"Eventually," Daddy tells him. "Sometimes communities help by bringing in more sand, but nature has a way of healing itself."

I can't wait much longer. "What about the sea turtles?" I cry out. "Are they okay?"

"Let's go see, Sassy." Grammy takes my hand and we run to the place where we first found the sea turtle nest. I almost don't know the spot. The large rock nearby helps me remember.

The hole where the eggs were first hiding is not there. Even the sand around it is gone. "Is this the place?" I ask Grammy.

"I think so, Sassy." She looks around as if she is not sure.

"The turtle eggs would be gone, right?" I'm almost shivering with worry and excitement.

"It's a good thing we moved them," Daddy says as he catches up with us. "That nest would not have survived the storm."

"You mean the little sea turtles would have been washed out to sea with the rest of the sand?" Sadora asks.

"Sadly, yes," Mom tells her.

"Let's climb up and check on the new nest," Poppy suggests.

My heart is beating fast as we get closer.

We climb up the rocks to the place where we moved the sea turtle eggs.

"Look, Sassy!" Sabin says with excitement. "Your lucky pink ribbon is still flapping in the breeze by the new nest."

"Amazing," Sadora says. "After all that wind." The hot-pink strip of fabric flutters like a proud banner. The green ribbon has disappeared.

We tiptoe to the place where the nest is hidden.

"It's safe and sound!" Daddy says. He sounds really happy. He checks under the sand and finds several of the eggs. They are warm and dry.

"I've got to call Michael and let him know," Poppy mumbles. "He'll be very glad."

"Are cell phones working?" Mom asks.

"Mine is!" Sadora answers with certainty. "I had to call all my friends at home and let them know we survived a hurricane!"

Everybody laughs. Sadora and her cell phone are never far apart.

"When will the little sea turtles hatch, Dad?" Sabin asks.

"In a few weeks."

"Because of us?" I ask.

"Yes, Sassy. We saved the turtles. They will go back to the sea and return here to make new nests."

"Way cool," I say.

"Let's head back to the house," Grammy suggests. "Who's ready for lunch?"

Sabin and Poppy both raise their hands. "Me!" they say at the same time.

"When do we go back to Ohio?" I ask Daddy.

"If the roads are clear and the airport is open, probably in a day or so," he replies.

"Will I have time to learn how to hammer before we leave?"

"Absolutely," Poppy tells me.

"Race you back to the house!" Sabin calls out to Poppy. They both take off running.

"Will there be time for another visit to the beach?" I ask Mom.

"We can walk on the beach, as long as you are wearing your beach shoes, but I don't want you kids to swim yet," Mom warns. "There is too much stuff floating around that might not be safe for little feet."

"Sabin's got big feet," Sadora tells her with a giggle.

We all laugh as we head back to the house.

I grab Grammy's hand as we walk by the ocean one last time. "I hope you had a good birthday, Grammy," I tell her.

"We saved some sea turtles, sang some songs, and slept on the floor through a storm. I'd say that it was a terrific day. The best birthday ever!" she says.

"Are you sorry you didn't have the band and the cake?" I ask her.

Grammy stops walking and bends down so she is even with me. She touches my face gently. "I wouldn't change one single thing," she tells me clearly.

"Hurricane birthdays are really exciting," I tell Grammy, "but next year, can we celebrate with just cake and ice cream instead of winds and storms?"

She stands, stretches, and laughs out loud. "Absolutely, Sassy! Absolutely!"

Here are some fun facts about hurricanes and sea turtles!

HURRICANES

Hurricanes are severe tropical storms that form in oceans. Evaporation from the seawater increases their power.

Hurricanes have winds of at least 74 miles per hour. When they come onto land, the heavy rain, strong winds, and powerful waves can damage buildings, trees, and cars.

A hurricane can be up to 600 miles across and have wind speeds of up to 200 miles per hour.

Hurricanes north of the equator rotate in a counterclockwise direction around an "eye." The center of the storm, or eye, is the calmest part.

The heavy waves are called a storm surge. Storm surges are very dangerous and a major reason why you MUST stay away from the ocean during a hurricane warning or hurricane.

Hurricanes have names, such as Hannah, Katrina, or Ike. They alternate between girl names and boy names. If a hurricane does a lot of damage, its name is never used again.

SEA TURTLES

Sea turtles are large air-breathing reptiles. They come in many different sizes, shapes, and colors.

Some sea turtles weigh less than 100 pounds; others can weigh up to 1,300 pounds!

Female sea turtles come ashore to the beach where they were born to lay their eggs in the sand. Males rarely return to land after crawling into the sea as hatchlings.

The hatchlings return to the sea sixty days after the eggs are laid on the beach. The mother does not stay to watch the nest or help the babies hatch.

Sea turtles face many hazards. Sharks, big fish, and circling birds all eat baby turtles. Also, many sea turtles die after accidentally eating plastic garbage. The obstacles are so numerous for baby turtles that only about 1 in 1,000 survives to adulthood.

The earliest known sea turtle fossils are about 150 million years old.

Destruction of the feeding and nesting areas where sea turtles live, along with pollution of the world's oceans, is taking a serious toll on sea turtle populations.

Sea turtles are in danger of extinction. But you can help by keeping our beaches clean and by working with sea turtle organizations that monitor them.